Timothy Turtle Mysteries
Complete Series
By Veronica Anderson

Illustrations by K. L. Robertson
Copyright © 2012 Veronica Lolonda Anderson
Smashwords Edition

For Darius, Ken, Anthony, Frank, Malichi and Arenthius.

Chapter One: Timothy Turtle In the Case of the Mysterious Shadow

Timothy Turtle had been solving mysteries at the Mystery Mode for as long as he could remember. But his most recent case was one that even the most experienced detective would have trouble solving. Simon Salamander had come to Timothy's home on a stormy night.

He said that for weeks he had been having trouble sleeping. He claimed that every night before bed, he would see a mysterious shadow on the outside of his window. Whenever he went outside to see what was casting the shadow, there would be nothing there. He asked Timothy if he would take his case. Timothy agreed. Still, he wished that Simon had come to him when he'd first sighted the shadow. Timothy sat in his thinking chair to figure out how he would capture the mystery shadow. "Hmm." he said to himself. Then he had it. He was going to camp outside Simon's window.

The sun came out early the next day. It was so hot that all of the rain from the night before quickly dried up. This was perfect. Timothy could start his investigation as soon as night fell. Timothy went to Slimy Snake's Hardware store to pick up all the supplies that he would need for his campout. Timothy pulled out his list. It read: camping bag, a tent, large flashlight, batteries, marshmallows, chocolate bars and graham crackers. As he shopped for his items, he thought about the fact that he was working. It didn't mean that he couldn't enjoy himself. Timothy had never camped alone. He decided to call in his assistant, Frankie Frog. Frankie had recently returned to town. He had been away doing research on another case. He seemed quite happy to go on a camping trip. That was until he found out that trip wasn't for having fun. They had to solve another case.

Timothy and Frankie set up their tents and made a campfire outside Simone's window. Simon came out and thanked Timothy again for taking his case. Simon was really tired and decided to go to bed. Timothy had instructed him to knock on the window when the shadow appeared. Simon got into bed. Then he looked over at the window. This time there was no shadow. He quickly fell asleep. Timothy and Frankie roasted marshmallows and melted chocolate as they waited for Simon to tell them if the shadow had appeared. It was getting really late. Timothy and Frankie decided to call it a night. Simon's problems seemed to be over. Because when Timothy peeked into Simon's bedroom window, he was fast asleep.

    That morning, Timothy awoke late. He saw that Frankie was gone. He decided to look around for him. He felt a sense of fear come over him. That was until he heard Frankie's voice coming from the inside of Simon's house. Timothy decided to go inside to join them. Simon looked very happy. He was telling Frankie how well he'd slept. He said that there hadn't been any sign of the shadow that night. He was so happy. He thanked Timothy for solving the case. Timothy sat down to eat breakfast with his friends. He thought to himself, "I didn't do anything." Timothy and Frankie packed up their things and went home. Timothy couldn't help but think about the shadow. He wondered why the shadow had chosen not to appear. In any case, Simon felt better and that's what really mattered.

    Simon went to bed early that night. He knew that he wasn't going to see the shadow. He had no fear of looking at the window, but when he did, he saw that the shadow was back. Simon was so afraid that he put his head beneath the covers. He didn't close his eyes all night. As soon as day broke, Simon went straight to

Timothy's house. When Timothy Turtle open the door, Simon looked very tired. He had dark circles around his eyes and he looked as if he could barely stand. Timothy helped him to the couch. "Are you all right?" Timothy asked him. Simon was so weak that he couldn't speak. Timothy gave him a warm glass of milk. He decided that he would fix Simon some breakfast. When he returned to the room, Simon was fast asleep. The case hadn't been solved, but Timothy knew exactly what he would do.

When Simon Salamander awoke, he told Timothy about what had happened when he'd gone to bed. He told him that the shadow had appeared once more. Timothy decided that he was going to spend the night at Simon's house. He asked Simon to stay at his house for the night. Simon agreed to stay because he really wanted the shadow to be gone. That night, Timothy and Frankie went over to spend the night at Simon's house. Timothy sat on Simon's bed and Frankie sat in a chair near the window. Sure enough, Timothy could see the shadow. It was right outside the window. He and Frankie ran outside but they didn't see anyone. There was only the moon and a large tree that stood in its path of light. It was then that Timothy figured out what the shadow was. He told Frankie to go inside. He tapped on the window and asked Frankie if he could still see the shadow. Frankie could still see it. It was simple. The moon had cast light down onto the tree's branches, which caused a shadow to be cast into Simon's bedroom window. The shadow hadn't appeared the night before because of Timothy and Frankie's campfire.

Simon was so happy to hear that the shadow was only a tree. He felt silly for being so afraid of a shadow. Timothy told him that there was no shame in being afraid of the unknown. After breakfast, Simon went home. Timothy Turtle had solved another case with the aid of his assistant, Frankie Frog. They were always happy to help a friend in need. That night when Simon Salamander went to bed, he wasn't afraid to look at the window. He thought that maybe he would see the shadow as a friend instead of something scary. Simon knew that it was all thanks to his friends. Timothy recorded the case in his journal. It was case number twenty four. He decided to call it: *The Case of Mysterious Shadow.*

Chapter Two: Timothy Turtle In the Case of the Missing Necklace

Greta Gecko had called to Timothy Turtle's office a total of five times that day. Each time she had left a message about her missing necklace. Timothy and Frankie Frog had just come back from a fishing trip. Tina Tortoise, Timothy's secretary, was tired and ready to go home. She gave Timothy the messages and told him that Greta Gecko was on her way to the office. This wasn't the first time that Timothy had worked with Greta. She had once lost a diamond ring. She'd thought that it had been stolen, but she had only misplaced it in her bedroom. Timothy put his fishing gear in a closet and returned to his office. When he stepped into the room, Greta Gecko was sitting there with tears in her eyes. Timothy asked her to calm down and tell him what had happened.

She said that she'd been out shopping and when she returned home, her necklace was missing. Timothy gave her a notepad and told her to write down all the places that she had been during the course of the day. Timothy figured that she had probably lost the necklace in one of the shops on Iguana Avenue. Greta took the pad then looked up at Timothy. "I didn't wear the necklace today." she exclaimed. She told Timothy that someone had came into her house and taken the necklace from her jewelry chest. Timothy decided to investigate at Greta's house.

When he walked through the door, the house looked fine. The living room looked exactly how it had looked the last time he had visited. He continued through the house and saw that the house didn't look like someone had broken into it. He asked Greta if she had locked the door before she left to shop. She said that she always locked her door. He looked into Greta's jewelry box, only to find that the box was still full of jewelry. Greta told him that the only thing that had been taken was her Three-Stoned Emerald necklace. She said that it had been given to her by her father for her birthday.

Timothy realized that something or someone else had to be involved. Why would someone see a jewelry box full of jewelry and only take one necklace? Why would they risk taking something from Greta's home in broad daylight? It was then that Timothy decided to talk with Greta's neighbors. He went over to Carl Cottonmouth's house and asked if he had seen anyone enter Greta's house. Carl said that he had only just returned home from work. He said that the only person he had seen at the house was Greta herself. He had no clues to give to Timothy.

Timothy crossed the road to Bertha Bullfrog's house. He knocked repeatedly, but she wasn't home. There was only Tiffany Tuatara left. She was Timothy's last hope. If she didn't have any information, he was going to be back at square one. He had checked the house and found no clue that anyone had broken into it. Could Greta have misplaced her jewels yet again? Timothy Turtle knocked on Tiffany's door. It took awhile for her to answer the door. She opened the door and invited Timothy inside. Timothy took a seat at her kitchen table. She said that she'd been baking all day. She was planning a bake sale. She talked so much that Timothy could barely get a word in.

Timothy finally got a few of his questions into the conversation. He asked her if she had seen anyone going into Greta's house today.

She said that she had been in the kitchen and could see Greta's front door. She said that no one had visited the house. It was then that Timothy noticed an Emerald necklace lying on the table. Timothy was shocked but decided to play it cool. He asked her in a calm voice, "Where did you get such a nice necklace?" Tiffany slowly turned and looked at Timothy. She explained that Greta owned the necklace and had loaned it to her the day before. She said that Greta was coming over later for tea and that she would return it to her then.

Timothy smiled and rose from the table. He was about to leave when Tiffany offered him a cupcake. He took the cake and left. He was surprised that it was really good. He was happy that no crime had been committed. He walked back to Greta's house and explained what had happened. It was then that she remembered. "Another case solved." Timothy said to himself as he traveled back to his office.

Chapter Three: Timothy Turtle In the Case of Terrible Tuesdays

There was always a terrible smell coming from the Chameleon Chuck Restaurant. It smelled especially bad on Tuesdays. The residents that lived on Crocodilian Street had had enough. They'd tried several times to talk to the owner but he never had time to talk to them. The restaurant was always full of customers. On Tuesdays, they offered a special variety of food. After the owner refused to talk to them, they decided to go to the mayor. Mayor Gila Monster realized that he really didn't have anyone that could investigate the smell that came from the restaurant. He decided that it would be best to hire Timothy Turtle.

Timothy had been planning a trip for weeks. He was going to visit his brother, Terrence. He had been under the weather for awhile. So Timothy was going to take care of him. The Croc Company sent a kart over for Timothy. He was soon on his way. When Mayor Gila Monster arrived at Mysterious Mode, there was only Frankie Frog and Tina Tortoise. He asked Frankie where he could find Timothy Turtle. Frankie informed him that Timothy had left town to take care of his brother. The major told Frankie that it was an emergency. He told them that some citizens had some complaints and he needed Timothy to handle a case for him.

Tina told the major that Frankie was Timothy's assistant and he could help him. The mayor really didn't know Frankie but he had to accept. He explained the problem to Frankie and Tina. After hearing the story, Tina explained to the mayor that she knew the owner of the restaurant and that she and Frankie would go and talk to him. The mayor was pleased and said that he had to go. Tina and Frankie went over to the restaurant. It wasn't open yet, so they went in through the back door. In the kitchen, they found the owner, Chuck, hard at work.

Tina went over to talk to Chuck. She told him about the complaints that people had about the restaurant. He said that it couldn't be helped. He said that the smell came from the different foods that he prepared. He explained that each dish had a pleasant smell, but it was just that when the smells combined, that they gave off a terrible odor; which led him to open the window; and let fresh air inside the restaurant. Tina had eaten there many times. She had an idea. She told Chuck that if he invited the residents, on the street to eat there; maybe they wouldn't complain so much. So Frankie and Tina went to every house on Crocodilian Street, to invite the residents to the restaurant.

That Tuesday night, amphibians from everywhere came to eat at Chuck's place. It was a success. They liked the food a lot. Once they tasted the food, they didn't have any more complaints. The mayor even came to enjoy the food. Two weeks had passed and there still weren't any complaints about the smells that came from Chameleon Chuck's Restaurant. When Timothy arrived, he asked Frankie if he'd missed anything. He said no but Tina laughed and said, "Only some really good food."

Chapter Four: Timothy Turtle In the Case of the Cruel Crocodiles

Sylvia Snake was just about fed up with nightly visits from vandals. Every morning she went out to her garden to find that more vegetables were gone. She had followed the advice of friends, to set traps for the vandals but she never caught anything or anyone. It was time to bring in a professional. She took out her *Amphibian Woods Scale Phone Directory*. Under the heading of detectives, she found Timothy Turtle's *Mystery Mode*. The things that were happening during the night, at her home, were definitely a mystery. She had to call. She was more than happy when Timothy said that he would be right over.

Timothy Turtle had never particularly like going to that part of the Amphibian Woods, but he had promised Sylvia that he would be right over. Frankie Frog, as usual, was nowhere to be found. "It looks like I'm alone on this one!" Timothy said to Tina Tortoise as he walked out the door. "Good luck boss. And be careful." Tina warned as the door closed behind Timothy. Everyone knew about the eastern area of the Amphibian Woods. It was just simply not a safe place. For this reason alone, Timothy wondered why a nice snake like Sylvia would ever take up residence there.

As Timothy traveled the path to Sylvia's home, he noticed that even in the daytime, the sunlight didn't pierce through the thick trees and bushes of the eastern forest. As Timothy walked deeper and deeper into the woods, he started to hear all sorts of noises and sounds. He couldn't decide which direction the noises were coming from. All he knew was that he could barely wait to get to the safety of Sylvia Snake's home. Finally, Timothy came out on the other side of the thick bushes to see a small yet beautiful cottage.

Sylvia was happy to see Timothy had arrived safely. She knew that many an amphibian could get lost in the woods. Sylvia offered

Timothy a drink and a slice of tomato pie before she began to tell him about her nightly visits from vandals. Before Timothy could finish his last bite of pie, he already had a plan to catch the mysterious vandals.

It would be night soon. He had to act fast. Sylvia had already told him that they came every night. So he wasn't worried about them coming. Timothy told Sylvia exactly what they would do. The only tricky part of the plan was that Sylvia would have to sit at the window facing her garden and watch. When Timothy gave her the signal, she would have to shine a light out the window. Timothy decided to rake up a bundle of leaves to hide inside. He saw the perfect spot beside and old oak tree in Sylvia's garden.

Night fell quickly. Timothy waited quietly. He knew that he couldn't make a sound least the vandals would run away. His patience paid off. In the distance he could hear footsteps and voices. "Chris, I'm not so sure about this. She's bound to figure out that it is us." a voice said beyond the trees. "Will you calm down? She doesn't know it's us. She would have said something by now Crystal." the other voice reassured. The footsteps stopped right in front of Timothy. He knew that this was as good a time as any to give Sylvia the signal.

Before the vandals knew it, leaves were flying up into the air and all around them. Sylvia recognized the leaves as Timothy's signal to shine the light. She did as she was told. Once the leaves had settled, there stood two young crocodiles in the spotlight. Sylvia gasped, "The twins!" "We're sorry, Ms. Snake!" they said in unison.

The twins knew that it was all over. They knew that Ms. Snake, their mother's best friend, wouldn't let this slide. Timothy led the two crocs inside. After Mrs. Croc arrived, Sylvia thanked Timothy for solving her little vandal problem. "No problem…I know that everyone needs a little help sometimes… no matter where they live." he said with a smile.

    After Timothy said his goodbyes, he closed the door to the cottage. Even in the distance, he could still hear the twins mother scolding them for vandalizing her best friends garden. He heard Sylvia say that they could have asked if they wanted veggies. Timothy laughed, "Another case solved… now if I could only make my way out of these woods… without getting lost."

Chapter Five: Timothy Turtle In the Case of the Mysterious Marsh Monster

Fishing at Gila Monster Marsh had always been the highlight of Manny Mongoose's weekend; that is until all the fish started disappearing. No matter what spot he chose to settle in, he still couldn't seem to catch any more than one or two fish. Manny loved fish but one or two fish wasn't going to feed his family of four for the whole week. He decided that he would call his old friend Timothy Turtle, to help him figure out where all the fish were going. After all, he knew the stories about there being a monster in the marsh couldn't be true. Timothy would figure things out.

Timothy Turtle decided that it would be nice to go on a fishing trip with his old friend Manny Mongoose. Things at the *Mystery Mode* were finally slowing down. If anything popped up, he knew that he could depend on Frankie Frog and Tina Tortoise to handle it. Taking the *Hare Line Express* was the fastest way to get to Gila Monster Mountain. After all, this was where Manny Mongoose had lived all his life. Timothy could remember the first time he'd met Manny, during a trip to visit his uncle Travis Turtle. They'd been good friends ever since then.

Manny Mongoose met Timothy at the *Hair Line Station*. Timothy Turtle could tell that something was bothering his old friend. "How are you Manny?" he asked in a cheerful tone. "Oh Timothy, it's terrible. I asked you to come here to help me figure out what's happened to all the fish in the marsh. If I can't catch fishes, my family doesn't eat." Manny explained. Timothy Turtle couldn't help but to think that maybe he wasn't going to be relaxing after all. "Well why don't you start from the beginning? Tell me when the fish started disappearing." Manny told Timothy that it had been three Saturdays since he'd had a decent catch at the Gila Monster Marsh.

He told Timothy that he was beginning to believe the stories about a monster being in the marsh. Timothy assured him that he'd get to the bottom of this mystery.

Timothy Turtle and Manny Mongoose made their way to the marsh. Timothy Turtle took a breath of the fresh air. The marsh looked and smelled the same as it did from when he was a kid. Manny and Timothy got into the boat and rowed to the middle of the marsh. They cast out their lines and waited. After an hour and a half, there still weren't any fish. They decided to try another spot. They cast their lines once more and waited. Still there wasn't one single fish. Manny was more worried than ever before. He knew that his wife was expecting him to bring fish for dinner. "Timothy, what are we going to do? Where do you think all the fish have gone?" Manny exclaimed. "There is definitely something going on. Don't worry Manny. I have a plan."

Timothy didn't believe in monsters. He figured out a long time ago that every mystery could be solved. That night, Timothy and Manny decided to camp in the woods near the marsh. Timothy Turtle had a feeling that the cause of the fish disappearances, were happening at night. He figured that all they had to do was wait. For hours, Timothy and Manny talked about the old times. Timothy noticed that Manny Mongoose had fallen asleep. He decided that he would put out the campfire and wait a bit longer.

Timothy was starting to get sleepy when he heard sounds coming from the marsh. He tapped Manny on the shoulder to wake him. "Manny, I hear something out on the marsh." "Is it a monster?"

Manny asked. "I don't think so." Timothy answered. He and Manny quietly made their way to the edge of the marsh. They could see a boat with a figure in it. Timothy couldn't tell who it was. Neither could Manny. "We have to get closer to see what going on. Follow me." Timothy whispered.

Timothy and Manny slid into the water. They swam close to the boat. Perhaps too close. The person on the boat couldn't see them. He threw a net right on top of Timothy and Manny. All they could do was yell for help. The net was taking Timothy and Manny deeper into the marsh. That was until strong arms pulled them both out of the water. All Timothy could remember was being cold and being covered by dry brush and bushes.

The next morning, Timothy Turtle awoke dry and warm. He could smell fish being cooked and hear Manny talking to someone. He looked around to see his old friend Manny sitting with an alligator. "Oh Timothy, you're awake." Manny said. "Yes, I guess I am." Timothy laughed. "This is Alec Alligator." Manny motioned to the gator next to him. Timothy smiled and shook his hand. After eating breakfast, Manny explained that Alec had been using nets to catch fish for himself and his large family. Alec Alligator explained that he hadn't known that anyone else fished at the marsh. He agreed to stop using nets and stick to using a pole. That way, there'd be plenty of fish for everyone.

Timothy waved goodbye to Manny Mongoose and Alec Alligator from the window of the *Hare Line Express*. He was happy that Manny Mongoose would have more than enough fish to feed his family. He looked down at the basket of fish that Alec had given him to take home. "What will I do with all this fish? Perhaps Frankie and Tina will want some. Oh well…. Another case solved." Timothy said as he waved goodbye one last time to his friends and Gila Monster Mountain.

Chapter Six: Timothy Turtle In the Case of Danger on Lizard Head Ridge

Timothy Turtle and Frankie Frog decided that today was a great day to climb the Amphibian Forest Mountain. They had been planning to do it for a very long time. The *Mystery Mode* was closed for the weekend. So there was no time like the present. Timothy gathered all his gear as did Frankie Frog. The elevation was high. That meant the higher they went, the colder it got. Frankie reminded Timothy to bring a jacket. They took the *Hare Line Express* to the Amphibian Natural Park, which is where the mountain was located.

When they got off the express, Timothy couldn't believe how many visitors were at the park. Frankie Frog was so excited that he didn't know what to do first. There were all sorts of trail line stores to visit. Stores for snacks made naturally, clothing made naturally and historical tours about the mountain. "Timothy, let's grab a snack before we start the climb." Frankie insisted. "We can have something to eat when we get to the top. It is a very long climb though… a snack sounds okay." Timothy agreed.

Frankie and Timothy went into a store called *Natural Honey Treats*. Timothy grabbed a few Honey-Leaf Bars, while Frankie Frog went for the Fly-Dip Honey Sticks. They both grabbed a bottle of Honey-Snap Juice to wash down their snacks. After eating, it was time to hit the trail. Walking the trail was fun. Timothy and Frankie saw a lot of their friends. Tina Tortoise was even there. She had her three grand-tortoises with her. Timothy was glad that he wasn't the one trying to control three little energetic turtles. He could almost remember how he was when he was a kid.

There were lots of teens on the trail. Timothy thought about how eager he was as a teen to fit in with his friends. He saw a crowd of teens leaving the trail. He knew that it was unsafe to do so. It was awfully easy to get lost in the mountains. It would be even harder to find someone if you didn't know where to look. Timothy called after them but they kept up their pace in the opposite direction. "I think those kids are going to be trouble." Timothy said to Frankie Frog as they watch the teens disappear behind the thick bushes. "Do you think we should follow them Timothy?" Frankie asked. "I think we should keep an eye on them. I remember when I was a teen. There was nothing that I wouldn't do to please my pals." Timothy explained as he and Frankie followed closely behind the teens.

There were four of them. As they got close, remembering to stay hidden, Timothy could see their faces. He recognized one of the young crocs. He was Chris Crocodile. Timothy wondered if Mrs. Crocodile knew where her son was. Timothy knew that Chris was sneaky at best. He and his twin sister, Crystal, had really did a number on Ms. Snake's garden. Was Chris up to no good with his friends? Timothy was curious to find out. The teens climbed further and further up the hill. Timothy and Frankie followed from a distance. "I think I know where their headed." Frankie whispered. "Where?" Timothy asked in a hushed tone. "I think they're going to Lizard Head Ridge." Frankie answered. "Hmmm. Why would they be going there? It's way too dangerous." Timothy exclaimed. Frankie pulled a face and hunched his shoulders.

Frankie was right about where he thought the boys had been headed. Sure enough, from the bushes where they hid, Timothy and

Frankie watched as the teens stood dangerously close to the edge. "You said that you weren't afraid to stand on the edge." Chris teased another croc. "I'm not afraid." the other croc yelled. "Then do it… cause if you want to hang with us, you can't be afraid of anything." Chris Croc goaded the other croc. Timothy hoped that the young croc wouldn't allow himself be talked into walking to the edge. He was sure to fall. Timothy decided that if he did, he and Frankie would have to stop him.

The croc was quiet. To Timothy, it seemed as if he would refuse. The young croc looked towards the edge of the ridge and started to walk. "Do it! Do it! Do it!" the other three crocs shouted. Before Timothy could get to him, the croc was standing on the edge. He looked nervous as he started to lose his footing. The other crocs rushed towards him but it was too much weight on the ridge. It started to give way. Timothy grabbed two of the crocs by the arm before they went over the cliff. Frankie scrambled and grabbed the other two. By the looks on their faces, the teens were more than happy to see Timothy Turtle and Frankie Frog.

After leaving the teens with the ranger, Timothy was a bit shaken. "If you hadn't suggested we follow those crocs, Frankie, those kids would have really got hurt today." Frankie glanced back in the direction where they'd left the scared crocs. "I was just thinking the exact same thing." Do you still want to climb that mountain or do you want to wait until next time?" Timothy asked in a brighter tone. Frankie looked at the mountain and then back at Timothy. "Are you kidding Tim… let's do this!" Frankie raved.

Timothy smiled and followed Frankie down the mountain path. He couldn't help but to think back to when he'd been young and so very eager to please… but he had never put himself or his friends in harm's way.

Have A Mystery Christmas
Timothy Turtle and the Christmas Tree Thieves

For the third week in a row, Timothy Turtle had received the same letter in the mail. The letters always said the same thing, "No Christmas in Amphibian Woods." Timothy still couldn't figure out why these unmarked letters were coming to the *Mystery Mode*. Then it finally happened. Nina Newt burst into the *Mystery Mode* and she didn't seem too happy. Nina Newt owned the farm where all the Christmas trees were grown for the town. "Timothy, I need your help." Timothy looked a bit shocked and asked, "What seems to be the problem?" "Someone's been stealing trees from the farm." Timothy offered Nina a seat and he listened intently as she told him about when the trees started to disappear from her farm.

From what Nina had said, Timothy determined that everything started happening at the farm at the same time he started receiving the strange unmarked letters. Someone wanted to stop Christmas from coming to the Amphibian Woods but who?" Don't worry Nina. Timothy Turtle is on the case."

Timothy Turtle pulled out his kit and headed over to *Holiday Harper*, Nina Newt's farm. Timothy decided to take a look around. He walked down the northern rows of trees, but nothing was a miss. Then he walked down the southern rows. The trees on this side were sparse. Timothy could see where the trees had been cut down and dragged. But dragged where? Another thing that caught his eye was the particular way the trees had been cut. Whoever had done this had not used a saw or a blade. It looked as if teeth or bite marks covered the breakpoints on the tree stubs. Timothy had an idea but he had to be sure.

That night Timothy Turtle and Simon Salamander crept back to the *Holiday Harper*. It was quiet but something didn't feel right. Timothy noticed that more trees had been cut and dragged. "Timothy, did you hear that?" Simon asked. "Yes." Timothy and Simon ran into the direction of the loud crash. Simon dropped his flashlight and looked down to pick it up. "We're on the path of the drag marks." Simon said. "I know. Simon, be careful. We're not alone here." Simon nodded his he'd and followed closely behind Timothy.

Timothy and Simon ran out onto the clearing. Trees were floating out on the water. They had been tied together with vines and were moving as if they were being pulled by some unseen force. Timothy and Simon Salamander followed the trees along the water's edge. Finally they came to a stop. Timothy and Simon braced themselves. Several beavers rose up out of the water. Timothy and Simon rushed towards them one of the beavers turned and saw them coming. "Look out." He yelled. Before Timothy and Simon could get to them, they jumped back into the water and swam away quickly. Timothy and Simon weren't a match for them in the water.

Timothy and Simon camped at the farm overnight. When daylight hit, Timothy Turtle couldn't believe his eyes. So many of the trees had been taken but he couldn't understand why the beavers would need so many trees. Who were the three beavers that he and Simon had encountered the night before? Why were they trying to stop Christmas from coming to the Amphibian Woods?

Timothy had to come up with a plan to capture the tree thieves' or there wouldn't be any trees left for the holiday. Timothy knew that the operation was somewhere on the river. They had to use water to move so many trees. Timothy Turtle, Simon Salamander and Nina Newt followed the Amphibian Waterway for almost two hours and there in the clearing they saw exactly what was going on. The beavers were building a massive den on the water. Timothy had never seen anything so big. It was tall and wide but why would the beaver need so much space? As Timothy, Simon and Nina got closer, their question was answered. Three female beavers and six small beavers came out of the massive structure. Timothy understood now but that didn't give them the right to steal from Nina Newt's farm. Why hadn't they just taken trees from this part of the forest? Timothy supposed that it was part of their plan to stop Christmas from coming to the Amphibian Woods.

"Why have you taken all these trees from my farm?" Nina Newt yelled. The beavers looked into the direction of Timothy and the others. "We don't have to answer your question. We live here peacefully." The largest beaver yelled back. "I think you do." Timothy proclaimed. "You three have broken the laws of the Amphibian Woods." Simon said as he braced himself for what was coming. "We have been here for years and watched you all celebrate as a community, never inviting us to join and never acknowledging our existence. Why should we care about your laws? And why should we care if you all don't have Christmas trees? We need the wood for our den." The beavers explained as they turned to enter their den.

"Daddy, why can't we have Christmas with them?" a young beaver asked. Everyone fell silent. It was then that snowflakes begin to fall. At first, they fell slowly then faster and harder. Timothy knew that if they didn't leave now, they'd be caught in the snowstorm. Timothy, Simon and Nina turned to leave the clearing. One of the female beaver called out to them, "You'll never make it back in time. Please come inside."

Timothy and the others followed the beavers inside the sprawling den. It was beautifully decorated with Christmas decorations and smelled of warm holiday meals. Timothy couldn't understand why they wanted to stop Christmas from coming and yet have their home be a perfect sentiment of the holiday.

"I know what you're thinking." The largest beaver spoke. Timothy turned to face him. "You all celebrate the season together, never coming here to wish us well. All we have is our family. We were all alone here. It's like we don't exist to you amphibians in town. So why should we care if you all are happy or not? Why should we care if you can't have Christmas?" Timothy took his words into consideration. The children waited for Timothy's response. "Christmas will come whether we have trees or not. It's a holiday that inspires the spirit of giving, not taking. Have you ever thought that no one knows that you all live out here? No one comes this far out in the woods." Timothy explained. Everyone looked to the largest beaver while one of the women served warm sap to Timothy, Simon and Nina.

The largest beaver was quiet for a while; then he burst out into a thunderous laughter. He had realized that Timothy had been right. He'd been sneaking in and out of town without anyone seeing him. His brothers hadn't dared to come near the town. "Can you ever forgive us?" he asked in a more solemn tone. Timothy looked at Nina Newt and she smiled. "Of course we can." She admitted softly. "The celebration will start in a few days in town. Won't you all come and get acquainted with rest of the amphibians in town?" Simon asked while extending his hand. "Yes, we will come. I'm Bury Beaver, this is my wife Beth. These are my brothers Billy and Bart, their wives, Bridget and Belinda. These are all our young ones, Becky, Benny, Bobby, Branden, Bernard, and Brisha." Everyone shook hands. After eating dinner, the snow let up and Timothy, Simon and Nina were able to go home. Timothy smiled as they dredged through the snow. "Another case solved" he thought "The Case of the Christmas Trees Thieves."

About the Author

Veronica Lolonda Anderson was born on February 11, 1979 in Lexington Mississippi. Her parents are Loretta and Frank J. Robertson Jr. She has nine siblings. Her childhood was spent in both Mississippi and Wisconsin. She graduated from Mississippi Valley State University in 2002 with a degree in History. While there, she received countless awards including President's Scholar and Honor Scholar. In 2005, she was awarded The Editor's Choice award from the National Library of Poetry and Poetry.com. She briefly attended graduate school during which she worked on a Masters in Criminal Justice. Before long, she was offered a job that would take her away from her studies. She currently resides in Mississippi where she incorporates technology during her work hours. In her leisure, she continues to write short stories, poems and songs. She also enjoys horror films, nature programs and science fiction movies.

Made in the USA
Columbia, SC
14 March 2022